CORTE MADERA 3\96

W9-BXX-928   1566 2446

FIESTA U.S.A.

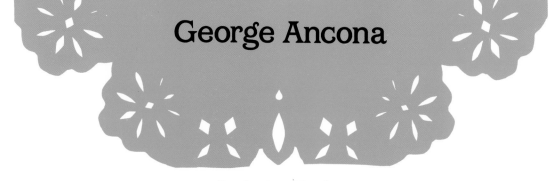

George Ancona

Lodestar Books

Dutton   New York

Copyright © 1995 by George Ancona

All rights reserved. No part of this publication may be reproduced or
transmitted in any form or by any means, electronic or mechanical, including
photocopy, recording, or any information storage and retrieval system now
known or to be invented, without permission in writing from the publisher,
except by a reviewer who wishes to quote brief passages in connection with a
review written for inclusion in a magazine, newspaper, or broadcast.

Library of Congress Cataloging-in-Publication Data

Ancona, George.
  Fiesta U.S.A. / George Ancona.
    p. cm.
  Includes bibliographical references.
  ISBN 0-525-67498-5
   1. Hispanic Americans—Folklore. 2. Hispanic Americans—Social life
and customs—Juvenile literature. 3. Festivals—United States—Juvenile
literature. 4. United States—Religious life and customs—Juvenile
literature. 5. United States—Social life and customs—Juvenile
literature. (1. Hispanic Americans—Social life and customs. 2. Mexican
Americans—Social life and customs. 3. Holidays. 4. Festivals.) I. Title.
GR111.H57A63 1995
394.2'61'08968076—dc20   CIP   AC   94-34828

Published in the United States by Lodestar Books, an affiliate of Dutton
Children's Books, a division of Penguin Books USA Inc., 375 Hudson Street,
New York, New York 10014

Published simultaneously in Canada
by McClelland & Stewart, Toronto

Editor: Rosemary Brosnan   Designer: George Ancona
Papel picado (cut paper) by Rosa María Galles
Printed in Hong Kong   First Edition   10 9 8 7 6 5 4 3 2 1

to Trini and Cordy Barnes

Gracias to the people who helped make this book:

In San Francisco, to Mía Galavez de González and her daughter, Gabriela Nicte González, who shared their celebration of the Día de los Muertos with me. And to María V. Piñedo of the Galería de la Raza.

In New Mexico, to Rudy Herrera, the master of ceremonies of the Matachines de El Rancho. Also to Barbara García and the children of the Pojoaque Elementary school, who gathered together to be photographed as the Matachines of Pojoaque, and to the dancers of Baila! Baila!

To Kathy and Lance Chilton of Albuquerque, who opened their home to friends and neighbors for the annual Posadas celebration. To Priscilla Pohl, for her delicious *bizcochitos*, and to her granddaughter Sandra, who took the part of María.

To Benjamin Salazar of New York's City Lore, for his help with the Three Kings' Day Festival. To Manuel Vega and Ignacio Villeta, for their cooperation in photographing the festivities in and around El Museo del Barrio.

Change goes on constantly, all around us. The seasons change, the weather turns, birds migrate, seeds are blown away from their parent plants. And so it is with people.

When Spanish-speaking people leave their homelands for this country, they bring their customs, foods, and fiestas. These are the festivals they hold to celebrate their holidays, and these they share with their neighbors. Fiestas bring the community together to commemorate an important event, to preserve a tradition—and to have fun. For the children of immigrants, fiestas offer a chance to experience a bit of what it was like for their parents growing up in the old country.

This book invites you to four fiestas that Hispanic people celebrate in the United States. Welcome, *bienvenidos*, may you have a wonderful time.

The barrio in San Francisco is bubbling with excitement. It is November 2, All Souls' Day. Today is the celebration of the Day of the Dead, El Día de los Muertos, the festival that honors friends and relatives who have died. It is a day to remember them and to celebrate life.

Annual festivals for remembering the dead have been celebrated by ancient civilizations of Egypt, Europe, and parts of Central and North America. Today, the Day of the Dead is celebrated in Mexico and in the United States by Mexican-Americans. In Mexico, families build altars in their homes and then join their neighbors in the town cemetery to decorate the family graves. In some towns, they spend the night there picnicking, singing, praying, and remembering their dead relatives and friends.

The store windows in San Francisco's barrio are filled with painted skeletons, marigolds—flower of the dead—and *pan de muertos*—sweet breads baked especially for the holiday. Children are given candy skulls of melted sugar that are inscribed with their names.

At home, people build an altar that displays photographs of friends and relatives who have died. On the altar, they place the dead people's favorite foods, toys, and other objects amid flowers and the image of the Virgin of Guadalupe, the dark-skinned patron saint of Mexico. Comical skeletons in everyday clothes, doing everyday things, are also placed on the altar. In public places, artists create special altars for the holiday.

Gabriela has made an altar in her home for a friend and family members who have died. On it she has included her friend's favorite toys, candies, and a written message to her.

Tonight is the big parade in the streets of the barrio, and Gabriela will take part in it. She wears a traditional Mexican dress. Her mother ties two huge silver bows into Gabriela's shiny, black, braided hair. Then she paints half of Gabriela's face white to look like a skull.

Gabriela, her mother, and their friend sell candles to the people who will walk in the procession. The Day of the Dead was originally celebrated only by San Francisco's Mexican community, but now people come from all over the city to march and to remember their friends and loved ones, many of whom have died of AIDS.

The musicians begin to play. The marchers light their candles, and the parade is under way. White skulls and bones glow in the darkness, which is filled with hundreds of flickering candles. Costumed stilt walkers dance and play instruments, while below them skeletons prance in the dimly lit streets. It is a carnival of living, joyous people united in their mockery of death.

The parade finally comes to rest in front of a stage. The marchers surround the stage to watch, applaud, and accompany the performers. A troupe of dancers in shimmering feathers performs Aztec dances of Mexico. So ends El Día de los Muertos—the Day of the Dead, or All Souls' Day—a festival that has its roots in antiquity and that has found a place among us here.

Christmas is near, and the nights of New Mexico are lit up with the warm glow of *farolitos*, brown paper bags with some sand in them that holds a shimmering candle. Towns are filled with rows of *farolitos* placed along streets and on buildings. In southern towns such as Albuquerque, the lights are called luminarias.

The processions of Las Posadas, which means "the inns," take place during the nine days before Christmas. Participants reenact Mary and Joseph's attempt to find lodging in Bethlehem. Some neighborhoods celebrate this fiesta for the entire nine days, others on just one night before Christmas. In this posada, the revelers are joined by many non-Hispanic neighbors, who have adopted the fiesta and take part every year.

In homes, kitchens are filled with the sweet smell of cinnamon and anise, as the traditional Christmas cookies called *bizcochitos* emerge from the ovens.

While her grandmother bakes *bizcochitos*, Sandra is dressed by her mother for her role as Mary. Children usually take the roles of Mary, Joseph, and the shepherds who accompany them. Long underwear, sweaters, and gloves will keep Sandra warm in the cold winter night.

Outside, neighbors gather together and light candles.
They all have a sheet of paper with the words to the song
they will sing in front of each house.

Mary rides a burro while Joseph and the shepherds walk at her side. The neighbors follow as they go to the nine houses that are taking part. A small group of singers enters the house while the others remain outside.

Those outside sing the first stanza of the song:

¿Quién les da posada	Who will give lodging
a estos peregrinos,	to these pilgrims,
que vienen cansados	who arrive exhausted
de andar los caminos?	from traveling the roads?

Then, those inside respond:

¿Quién es quien la pide?	Who is it that asks?
Yo no le he de dar	I shall not give it
si serán ladrones	should you be robbers
que quieren robar.	who wish to steal.

At each house, they sing a different request and denial. This year, Joseph insists on having a turn at riding the burro, so Mary has to walk to the last house.

When the procession reaches the ninth house, they sing

No tengáis en poco	Do not belittle
esta caridad:	this charity:
El Cielo benigno,	Benevolent Heaven,
la Reina del Cielo.	the Queen of Heaven.

Those inside respond:

Ábranse las puertas,	Open the doors,
rómpanse los velos;	tear off the veils;
que viene a posar	who comes to lodge
la Reina del Cielo.	is the Queen of Heaven.

The hosts sing, *"Entren, santos peregrinos"*—"Enter, holy pilgrims"—upon which the door swings open and the chilled singers are invited in. A potluck dinner and trays of *bizcochitos* with hot chocolate await them.

After dinner, the children go out to the backyard to break the piñata. Each takes a turn hitting the swinging piñata with a stick. Finally, after a mighty blow, the piñata bursts open, scattering candy. The children scamper to pick up the sweets. They continue their search by candlelight until the very last piece is found.

It's late, and parents gather their children and go home. Once again, Las Posadas brings neighbors together to share in a traditional fiesta and the warmth of friendship.

It is New Year's Day in the tiny village of El Rancho in northern New Mexico. Down the dirt road comes a group of strangely costumed figures led by a masked man with a whip in his hand. He is called *el abuelo*, the grandfather, and he shouts to the waiting crowd that the dance of Los Matachines is about to begin. The *abuelo* explains to the crowd:

> We think Los Matachines originated around the time the Moors invaded Spain in the eighth century. The Spanish conquistadores brought it here, but no one knows for sure how the dance began. It has been performed in both Indian pueblos and Hispanic towns since the sixteenth century.

When he finishes his introduction, *el abuelo* snaps his whip and the musicians begin to play.

The dance begins with the entrance of the principal dancer, *el monarca*—the king— accompanied by *el abuelo*, La Malinche, *el torito*, and the Matachines. The Matachines represent the arrival in Mexico of Hernán Cortés, the Spanish conqueror of the Aztecs. In their right hand the Matachines carry a rattle and in their left, a *palma*, a three-pronged fan that represents the Holy Trinity.

The *abuelo* introduces a little girl dressed in white to the *monarca*. She is called La Malinche, the Aztec princess who converted to Catholicism and became the interpreter for Cortés. Her dance among the Matachines depicts the arrival of Christianity in the New World.

One or more *abuelos* provide comedy and ensure that the
spectators are part of the dance by stealing their shoes and
handbags—or even their children. The crowd roars with
laughter as the *abuelo* runs through the dancers chased by
a giggling or angry bystander. Spectators often pin money
on the dancers as offerings.

An *abuelo* brings in *el torito*, a little boy dressed as a bull. The *abuelos* tease the bull while he chases and butts them. La Malinche drops a handkerchief, which the *torito* picks up. She pulls the handkerchief away and the *abuelos* subdue the *torito*.

Another boy dressed as a *monarca* dances alongside the group. He is an apprentice who will someday perform the role of *monarca*.

To keep the tradition alive for the next generation, the nearby elementary school organizes a children's Matachine group. Parents make the elaborate costumes and teach the children the ancient steps their elders do.

As in the adults' performance, the *abuelo* kneels down to pay respect to the *monarca*. All the Matachines then kneel and extend their *palmas* so that they touch one another. The *monarca* leads La Malinche as they dance over the *palmas*.

Back at El Rancho, the dancing ends when the musicians play a march and the performers leave. The crowd breaks up to eat, drink, and dance as the fiesta continues throughout the day. Mexican folk dances are also performed. And so the history and beliefs of the Hispanic people of the Southwest are celebrated and live on through the dance of Los Matachines.

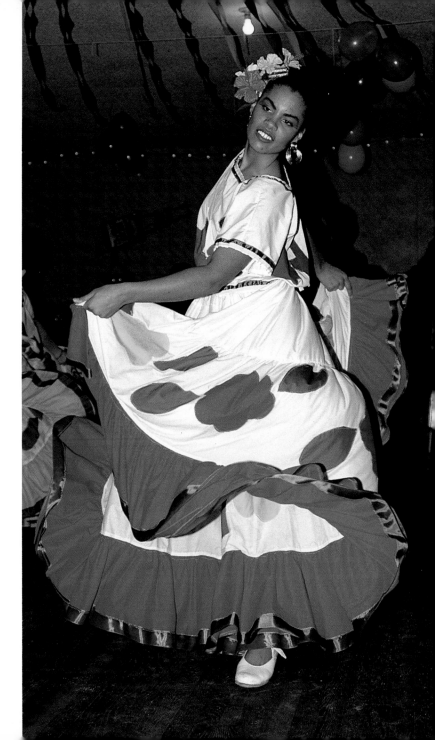

It is January 6, Three Kings' Day in East Harlem—the barrio in New York City.

Twelve days after Christmas, La Fiesta de los Reyes Magos celebrates the three wise kings who came bearing gifts for the Christ child.

Instead of hanging stockings by the chimney, last night the children of the barrio put grass and water in a shoe box under their beds for the camels or horses of the three kings. The children hope the three kings will leave gifts.

The big city is bitter cold, not at all like the tropical lands in the Caribbean that their families come from. Gusts of snow turn cheeks and noses red. Outside the Museo del Barrio, men are struggling to put together giant puppets representing the three kings.

Around the corner, schoolchildren arrive with cardboard figures of the three kings. Bundled up against the cold, the children wear paper crowns and white angel's robes over their hats and coats.

A musical group called El "Funky" Jíbaro climbs into an open truck, and while the snow falls on them they begin to play and sing traditional Puerto Rican songs. As the truck moves down the street, people on the sidewalk fall in behind it. They shake maracas, play the *güiro*, and break into spirited dancing.

Behind come the three wise men—Melchior, Balthazar, and Gaspar—each carrying a little gift box. Groups of schoolchildren, many of whom are dancing, follow the three kings. The parade is under way.

Giant puppets of the three kings tower over the marchers, who are getting wet from the falling snow. Those watching the parade on the sidewalks let out a chorus of *Oooo*'s as the three camels and the burro pass by.

After a two-hour parade through the barrio, the marchers return to the Museo del Barrio. El "Funky" Jíbaro plays for the children. Some of them leap into the aisles to dance. When the music stops, the audience grows quiet and the story of the three kings is told.

This is the story: Long ago, there were three wise kings who on a cold winter night saw a star shining brighter than any other in the sky. This was the omen of the birth of Jesus. To the first king, Melchior the dark, came a hermit who gave him gold to take to the child. To the second, Balthazar, the black king, a blind man brought myrrh. And to the third, Gaspar, the fair one, an orphan offered frank-incense. The kings, riding richly covered camels, met along the way. They followed the star, which led them to Bethlehem, where they saw the newborn babe in a manger. Kneeling before him, they gave him the gifts.

On their return, the kings were met by the hermit, the blind man, and the orphan. Each asked if the kings had brought back any gifts. Miraculously, when the kings opened their saddlebags, the bags contained three times more gold, myrrh, and frankincense than the kings had given away. It is told that the three kings continue their journey today, giving children gifts from their saddlebags.

When the story ends, the three kings come to the orchestra pit, which is piled high with toys, and give a gift to each of the eager children. So ends another Three Kings' Day in the barrio.

GLOSSARY

abuelo (ah-*bway*-loh) grandfather

barrio (*bah*-ree-oh) neighborhood, district

bienvenido (bee-en-bay-*nee*-doh) welcome

bizcochito (bees-koh-*chee*-toh) small cookie

conquistador (kon-*kees*-tah-dor) a leader in the Spanish conquest of the Americas

farolito (fah-roal-*ee*-toh) small lantern; a Christmas lantern consisting of a candle set in sand inside a paper bag

fiesta (fee-*es*-tah) festival

gracias (*grah*-see-ahs) thank you

güiro (*gwee*-roh) gourd used as musical instrument

jíbaro (*hee*-bah-roh) Puerto Rican peasant

luminaria (loo-mee-*nah*-ree-ah) (See *farolito*)

monarca (mo-*nahr*-kah) monarch, ruler

muerto (*mwayr*-toh) dead; a dead person

museo (moo-*say*-oh) museum

palma (*pahl*-mah) palm tree; palm of the hand

pan (pahn) bread

peregrino (pay-ray-*gree*-noh) pilgrim

piñata (pin-*yah*-tah) a hanging container that is filled with candy or other treats

posada (poh-*sah*-dah) inn

pueblo (*pway*-bloh) a Native American village in the Southwestern United States

santo (*sahn*-toh) saint

toro (*toh*-roh) bull